between

beside

above

joy

behind

with

below

T H E
FRIENDS
of the
Beverly Hills
Public Library

AROUND
the House
the Fox
Chased the Mouse

To Tom, Yukiko, Marina, and Niina — *across the sea, on our minds, in our hearts.* — R.W.

All my love to my wife Debbie (Biddy) and to Melissa (Bee), Danny (Billy), and Stephen (Cheeves) Bradshaw. — J.B.

First Edition
10 09 08 07 06   5 4 3 2 1

Text © 2006 Rick Walton
Illustrations © 2006 Jim Bradshaw

Published by
Gibbs Smith, Publisher
P.O. Box 667
Layton, Utah 84041

1.800.748.5439 orders
www.gibbs-smith.com

Designed and produced by Jim Bradshaw / www.jbradshaw.net
Printed and bound in Hong Kong

Library of Congress Cataloging-in-Publication Data
Walton, Rick.
Around the house, the fox chased the mouse : a prepositional tale / Rick Walton; illustrations by Jim Bradshaw.—1st ed.
   p.cm
Summary: A persistent fox chases a mouse all around the farm before finally catching it.
   ISBN 1-4236-0006-1
[1. Foxes—Fiction. 2. Mice—Fiction.] I. Bradshaw, Jim, ill. II. Title.
PZ7.W1774Ar 2006
[E]—dc22
                    2006003275

AROUND
the House
the Fox
Chased the Mouse

A Prepositional Tale

Written by Rick Walton

Illustrated by Jim Bradshaw

Gibbs Smith, Publisher
Salt Lake City

Around
the house the fox
chased the mouse...

BAAAAAAAAAA!

under
the fence,

beneath the tractor,

across
the field,

M

OooOooOooOooOOO

beside
the river,

up
the tree,

the branch,

between the signs,

PICK
PU

and **over** the rocks,

until...

"Tag! You're it!"

Then **over** the
rocks the mouse
chased the fox...